Ridley's Tale
A Turtle's Adventure

Written and illustrated by

Cynthia A. Coffin

Cynthia A. Coffin

ISBN-13: 978-1985652620
ISBN-10: 1985652625

DEDICATION

This book is dedicated to the workers and volunteers in hundreds, if not thousands, of organizations all over the world who work tirelessly to aid wounded, stranded, and endangered animals. Without their help many species would be even closer to extinction and generations to come would never see a Right Whale, an Olive Ridley turtle, a Black Rhino, an Orangutan, an Asian Elephant, or Giant Panda in the wild; and these are only a few of the species on the endangered list. On Cape Cod, where I live, organizations like the National Marine Life Center and IFAW's Cape Cod Stranding Network spend countless hours rescuing and rehabilitating sea turtles and seals in order to return them to the wild. We and our future generations owe them our support and our thanks.

Ridley's Tale

A Turtle's Adventure

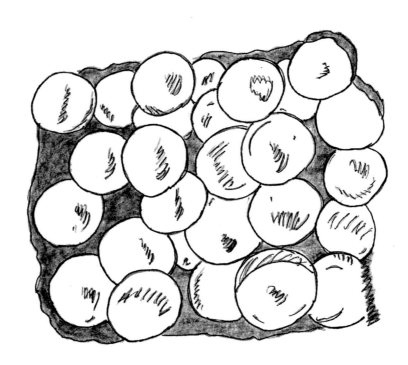

Little Ridley's life started as an egg on a sandy beach;

With a deep blue ocean just out of reach.

At first there was the egg and it started to crack;

And then out came little Ridley with a shell on his back.

He had two big front flippers and two smaller behind.

He felt rather awkward, but he tried not to mind.

He pushed to the left and he pushed to the right;

And just to move forward took all of his might.

He saw others around him all moving the same;

He felt so confused until he heard his name.

"Hey Ridley, come join us, we're going to sea;

It's just a short distance so come follow me."

So Ridley pushed forward, moving sand as he went.

By the time he reached water, his strength was all spent.

But the others, they coaxed him, "Come on Ridley, it's fun.

In the water it's easy; the hard stuff's almost done."

So Ridley pushed with his flippers and pulled himself thru the sand;

And in less than a minute he had left that dry land.

The ocean caressed him, he floated with ease.

With hardly a movement, he could drift with the breeze.

Then he learned if he pushed and held his breath in real tight,

He could dive 'neath the surface, then swim back up to the light.

All the others swam 'round him as they moved far from shore.

He saw whales in the distance and he watched seagulls soar.

They came upon floating algae and found things they could eat;

Small animals and plants that tasted oh so, so sweet.

Soon the sun in the sky started to sink toward the sea.

The turtles needed to rest, but where would that be?

The elders corralled them and said "Follow this way.

We need to find shallows; we're done for this day."

So they all swam together, some fast and some slow;

And they soon reached the coastline, with the moon all aglow.

They rested their bodies with their bellies so full.

The warm water lapped a lullaby with the tide's push and pull.

Sleep overtook them, and they dreamed of this day

That they discovered the ocean that would take them away

From the place of their birth to new places, unseen;

Of skies full of azure and seas of blue-green.

Little Ridley, among them, was soon lost in the dream

And a smile crossed his face, in the magic moon beam.

He thought of the joy he'd had since his birth;

And he offered his thanks for his place on this Earth.

The next day Ridley woke to quite a loud commotion.

All the turtles were startled by something in the ocean.

They saw it far off; this thing that floated in the sea.

They watched it grow larger; Ridley didn't know what it might be.

The elders gathered the young and said, "There's no need for alarm.

It's just a boat full of land dwellers; they mean us no harm.

Every month they pass by here; their journey's not just a whim.

They come to this bay to join us as we swim. "

Sure enough in a short time the boat stopped not far away;

And creatures with black, shiny skin and flippers joined them in play.

The seal-like things dove to the reef with shiny shells on their backs;

And bubbles rose from their heads, lifting in disappearing stacks.

Ridley felt brave and swam near but the two-legged thing grabbed on tight.

Ridley panicked and tried to dislodge it; but it held on with such might.

They both raced through the sea, then at once the thing let go.

Ridley kept on swimming to get away from this odd, clinging foe.

Ridley's Tale

Ridley hid watching the beings swim while his friends showed no fear;

But Ridley was certain he'd had enough and vowed not to go near.

When the seal-like things went to the surface he left his hiding place

To hear his friends' tales of swimming with this two-legged race.

Ridley said the others were braver; he was content with his kind.

He'd just swim with his friends; not any others they'd find.

So the days turned to months as they travelled together.

They basked in the sun and endured stormy weather.

They swam and they drifted; the currents carried them East.

They often stopped along the coastline to rest and to feast.

The elders travelled by memory along paths once explored.

The youngsters enjoyed new adventures and never were bored.

Over the months Ridley and the others grew healthy and strong.

They swam in warm currents; never stopping too long.

Ridley noticed the sun shining lower as the days quickly passed.

The water seemed colder; the dark came so fast.

The elders seemed worried and huddled discussing their plight.

Swimming was no longer easy and that just wasn't right.

Everyone seemed to swim slower and grew more tired each day.

The elders knew the colder water was what stressed them that way.

"We need to keep going," one said. "The weather's changed much too fast.

If we don't get to warm waters; I'm not sure we'll all last."

So the turtles swam onward though they struggled with each stroke.

They were tired and hungry and at last one of them spoke.

"I can go on no further, I'm sorry to say.

I just have to rest then I'll be back on my way."

The elders were angry, "No that is a deadly mistake.

We have to keep swimming. We can't take a break."

But the tired youngsters and Ridley headed off towards the shore.

The water grew even colder; biting winds stressed them more.

Ridley's Tale

And in one awful moment Ridley knew a mistake had been made.

He felt the cold overtake him; he was frozen where he stayed.

He could not move his flippers; he felt stuck in the sand.

He felt confused and so dizzy; there was no relief on dry land.

"Go back," he yelled to those swimming, "this beach is no where to be."

"Follow the elders to safety. Please don't follow me."

Then his vision grew dimmer; breathing was harder to do.

He felt his consciousness slipping till darkness was all that he knew.

Later Ridley woke to unfamiliar surroundings; he felt alone and afraid.

He missed the ocean, the elders, and the friends he had made.

Then suddenly he remembered how he'd felt on the beach.

The cold, and the wind, the life he'd known -- out of reach.

Wherever he was, he knew that he had been saved.

There was algae to dine on and all the warm water he craved.

As his vision grew clearer, he saw more turtles near by.

He called out their names till they gave a reply.

They were all so very happy that none were lost to the cold.

Then Ridley saw a two-legged creature and felt rather bold.

He swam up to the glass and gave the creature a smile.

He could swear it smiled back; then it disappeared for awhile.

It came back rather quickly and walked up to his tank;

And threw Ridley a fish, that he ate before it sank.

The fish kept on coming; he ate one, then two more.

He dove up and down and was content to his core.

Day by day he grew stronger; he saw his friends do the same.

He found the two-legged things were quite gentle; they seemed rather tame.

Two-legged things had once scared him so very much;

But these were loving and caring with kind words or a touch.

Then one day there was excitement; everyone was hurrying around.

He was lifted out of his tank and put in a crate on the ground.

Then they lifted him up; he had no time to react.

Something momentous was happening; Ridley knew that was a fact.

Soon he and the others were taken outside

And placed in a moving thing; they were taking a ride.

After what seemed like forever they were on a boat in the sea.

They could feel the movement on the water and they longed to be free.

One two-legged thing lifted Ridley; for a moment he hung in mid air.

Then he was placed in the water; his friends were already there.

They all felt such emotion and were sad to be saying goodbye.

The two-legged things were waving and smiling, and some started to cry.

Ridley too felt a sadness; though he felt joy here in the sea;

For he knew he was finally back where he needed to be.

So he and the others turned with one last look back to the boat;

And some dove deep into the ocean; while others decided to float.

Later they gathered together and tried to plan what to do;

An older turtle said, "We need to swim west; my sense of direction is true."

So they followed the elder, and swam and ate as before.

And after weeks of this journey they were back home on their shore.

The other turtles were disbelieving when they saw their return.

"How did you ever make it and what did you learn?"

Ridley happily told them how they were able to survive;

And of the two-legged creatures who had kept them alive.

"And I learned something greater than any lesson before.

That creatures who may seem different and scary can be so much more."

"And I vow from here forward not to judge with a glance;

For friends can come in all shapes and sizes; if we just give them the chance."

Cynthia A. Coffin

ABOUT THE AUTHOR

Cynthia Coffin has been writing rhyming poetry since she was in grade school. Friends and family members have been the recipients of her creations throughout the years. Though she worked for thirty years in the Public Health Field, writing, music, and drawing are the things that have always brought her great joy and fulfillment. Now her dream is to touch others' hearts with her poetry and stories; to make people stop and think about all the beautiful gifts of this Earth, and to pay attention to the ways of Nature that can teach us to be better humans. For the last 20 years she has created personalized poetry and greeting cards. In 2015 she finally realized a dream come true when she self published her first book of her favorite original poems and photographs, "It's the Little Things That Matter." She then went on to publish two illustrated children's books. The first is "Parada's Rainbow" the tale of a little filly who dreams of owning a rainbow and her journey to discover what dreams can accomplish. Her second book "Not Just a Tree", written in rhyming poetry, tells the story of the a tree's worth in the aftermath of its destruction and teaches the lesson that all of us are more than "Just" any one thing. This third book, Ridley's Tale, grew out of Ms. Coffin's love of nature and her support for wildlife rescue and rehabilitation organizations. She has been lucky enough to see first-hand the rehabilitation efforts of the National Marine Life Center near her home on Cape Cod. She also praises the work done by the Cape Cod Stranding Network and IFAW. She hopes that children will learn to love and respect all creatures in nature and in doing so will learn that all living things need to be protected and revered. In her personal life she is surrounded by loving friends, her father, and her beloved pets. Though her mother is no longer with her, Ms. Coffin knows that she looks down with loving approval on the work in this second chapter of her daughter's life.

Made in the USA
Middletown, DE
12 April 2018